POKÉMON DETECTIVE PIKACHU

SUPER SLEUTH

Adapted by Kate Howard

Scholastic Inc.

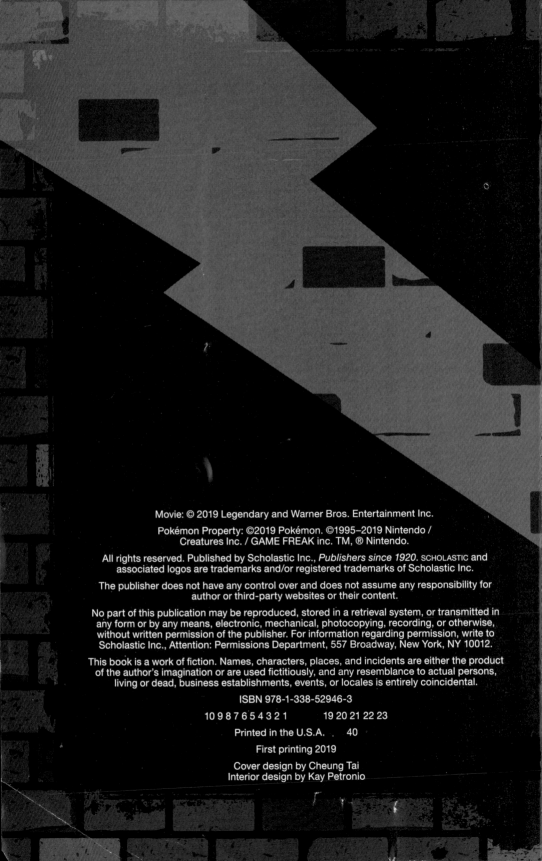

ISBN 978-1-338-52946-3

10 9 8 7 6 5 4 3 2 1   19 20 21 22 23

Printed in the U.S.A.   40

First printing 2019

Cover design by Cheung Tai
Interior design by Kay Petronio

SUN glinted off the morning dew as Tim Goodman and his friend Jack wandered through a quiet forest. "You hear that?" Jack whispered.

Tim peeked over a clump of tall grass. "A Cubone," he groaned. "We're not catching you a Pokémon, are we?"

"That is the *perfect* Pokémon for you," Jack told Tim, wiggling a Poké Ball in the air. "Water type is not right for you. Neither is Fire type. But Cubone is—"

Tim rolled his eyes. "Lonely."

TIM

"Jack, I'm not looking for a Pokémon," Tim said, leading his friend out of the forest. "I've told you this." He pulled out his cell phone. "Wait, five voice mails? Why would I have five voice mails?"

Listening to the messages, Tim's face grew serious. "It's the Ryme City Police Department," Tim told Jack. "There was an accident . . . my dad is dead."

While Tim rode a train to Ryme City, he thought about how sad it was that he and his dad had never been close.

Now Tim would *never* get a chance to know his father better. He sighed.

As the train pulled into the station, televisions played a message from the city's founder, Howard Clifford, and his son, Roger. "Here in Ryme City, humans and Pokémon live side by side. No battles, no Trainers, no Poké Balls. Ours is a stronger, more harmonious world."

Tim stepped out of the train into the strange, bustling city crowded with both Pokémon and humans living side by side.

RYME CITY

At the police station, a Snubbull greeted Tim inside Lieutenant Yoshida's office. The Pokémon glanced up at Tim. *"Snubbull,"* it grunted. It was obviously Lieutenant Yoshida's Pokémon partner.

"Hi, Tim," Lt. Yoshida said. "Your dad was the best of the best. It was a terrible tragedy losing him and his partner."

"His partner?" Tim asked.

"His Pokémon," Yoshida said.

Tim didn't even know his dad had *had* a Pokémon partner.

SNUBBULL

"How come you don't have a Pokémon?" Yoshida asked. "Your dad—Harry—said you wanted to be a Pokémon Trainer when you were young."

"Yeah, that didn't really work out." Tim took a deep breath. "Do you have the spare keys for his apartment? I should go wrap things up there."

LT. YOSHIDA

Yoshida handed him a set of keys. "Tim," he began gently. "Your dad loved you more than anything else in the world."

Tim gave him a grim smile. "It was nice to meet you, Lieutenant."

At his father's building, as Tim stopped to grab his dad's mail, he heard a rustling sound behind him. Tim spun around and looked down to find a Psyduck.

"*Psyduck*," the Pokémon blurted. "*Psyduck, psyduck, psyduck.*"

Tim sighed. "Are you trying to rob me, or just annoy me?"

"*Psyduck!*" the Pokémon repeated.

A young woman emerged from the shadows. "He's with me," she told Tim. "I've been waiting to see who would open up that mailbox. You and I need to talk."

PSYDUCK

"Who are you?" Tim asked.

"Lucy Stevens," she said, arching an eyebrow. "Reporter for CNM. I'm gonna need you to tell me everything you know about Harry Goodman. He was onto something big, then all of a sudden, his car crashes over a bridge? Something's rotten, and I'm gonna get to the bottom of it."

Tim pushed past Lucy. "I barely knew the guy. I haven't seen him in years."

Lucy called after him. "I can smell a story, and I'm going to find it!"

Upstairs, Tim looked around his dad's apartment. The walls were filled with awards for Harry's police work. Every surface was crowded with paperwork.

Under a newspaper clipping about the "ANCIENT MEW," Tim spotted a glass vial filled with purple liquid. Tim accidentally popped open the cap and released a cloud of purple gas.

"What *is* that stuff?" he gasped, coughing, and opened a window to release the awful cloud. Some Aipom were nearby.

Tim continued to explore. Suddenly, he was startled by a noise in the living room. "Hello?" Tim said. "Is someone there?"

A yellow blur darted across the floor, knocking over a lamp. "Ow, that's a sprain!" A low voice moaned.

Panicked, Tim searched for a weapon. He grabbed a stapler. "Whoever you are," he said in a shaky voice, "I know how to use this."

A small figure stepped out of the shadows. "Oh, it's a Pikachu!" Tim grinned. "Hey, little guy. How did you get in here?"

The Pikachu had on a detective hat. He looked up at Tim. "I know you can't understand me," the Pokémon said in a growling voice. "But put down the stapler or I will electrocute you."

Stunned, Tim dropped the stapler. "Did you just . . . talk?" he gasped.

The Pokémon sucked in a breath. "Whoa. Did you just . . . understand me?"

Tim's eyes went wide. "No. No, no, no."

"I need your help. I'm in serious trouble," Detective Pikachu told him.

"I'm gonna throw up." Tim said. He turned to the window—but found himself face-to-face with an angry Aipom.

Detective Pikachu glanced at the Aipom and took a step back. "That Aipom don't look right." Just as he said it, dozens of crazed Aipom flooded through the open window . . . and attacked Tim and Detective Pikachu! The purple gas had made them go mad!

"OH MY GOSH!" Detective Pikachu screamed. "C'mon kid, let's move!"

AIPOM

Tim and Detective Pikachu ran through the hall and out to the roof. The Aipom grabbed at Tim's feet. They pulled off his shoes.

Detective Pikachu led Tim across the roof, straight to a garbage chute. "We're jumping down here," he ordered.

Tim took a deep breath and jumped.

"Way to stick the landing, kid," Detective Pikachu said, grinning at Tim.

From the bottom of the dumpster, Tim and Detective Pikachu glanced up. The Aipom had all begun to return to normal, acting peaceful and calm once again.

"Huh. That was weird . . ." Detective Pikachu said.

"Why were you inside my father's apartment?" Tim asked.

Detective Pikachu gasped. *"You're* Harry's son?" He pulled off his hat and held it out. A tag inside said: IF LOST, RETURN TO: HARRY GOODMAN.

Tim stared at him, stunned. *"You're* Harry's Pokémon partner?"

Tim and Detective Pikachu sat down at a coffee shop to talk. Detective Pikachu told Tim that he had recently woken up in the middle of nowhere and couldn't remember anything. "The only clue to my past is Harry's name and address inside this hat," Detective Pikachu said. "I need to find Harry. He's the key to my past."

"Well," Tim said. "I've got some bad news for you. Harry's dead."

"What? No," Detective Pikachu said. "Did they find his body? Because if *I'm* still alive and kicking, that means Harry's still out there, too."

"I'm gonna go," Tim said, shaking his head. The police had told him his dad was dead—that was that. "We're done here."

"But wait!" Detective Pikachu chased after him. "We're gonna need each other."

"No," Tim snapped. "We don't. I don't need a Pokémon. Period."

"Then what about a world-class detective?" Detective Pikachu smiled. "Look, you can talk to humans, I can talk to Pokémon, and *we* can talk to each other. Magic brought us together, and that magic is called hope. Hope that Harry is still alive!"

Detective Pikachu convinced Tim that they had to figure out what had *really* happened to Harry. Detective Pikachu also hoped he might find information that would help him remember his own past. The pair returned to Harry's apartment to look for clues.

"Look what I found," Detective Pikachu said.

He handed Tim the small vial Tim had opened earlier. Tim could now see it was labeled with the letter *R*. "I smelled this on those Aipom when they attacked us yesterday," Detective Pikachu said.

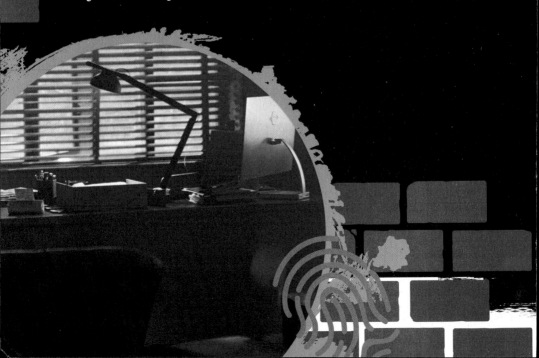

There was something suspicious about whatever was in that glass vial. They needed to figure out what it was—and what it had to do with Harry.

"I met someone yesterday who might be able to help us," Tim said. "A reporter at CNM. She was doing a story on Harry. I think she knows more than she let on."

Detective Pikachu climbed onto Tim's shoulder. "Let's go, kid!"

LUCY

"What are you doing here?" Lucy asked as soon as she spotted Tim and Detective Pikachu at her office. "Hey, you found yourself a Pokémon partner? He's cute!"

"Not exactly . . ." Tim said. "Listen, I found something in my father's desk. Nearly choked me to death." Tim held up the vial labeled *R*.

Lucy's eyes widened. She pulled a matching glass vial from her desk. "I heard your father had an informant near the docks. I went there to snoop around, and found this."

Tim and Detective Pikachu set off for the deserted docks of Ryme City. As they crept through the dark, Tim spotted a shadow moving on the side of a building. He stopped. "What is that?"

Detective Pikachu rubbed his stomach. "Silent but deadly. Apologies. My tummy's bad from all the coffee."

Tim shoved Detective Pikachu off his shoulders. "No, get off. I meant *that*."

MR. MIME

"It's a Mr. Mime. I think he recognizes you," Tim said.

"Well, I would've been with Harry—" Detective Pikachu broke off suddenly as he realized something. "Harry's informant is a Pokémon!"

They caught up to the Mr. Mime and asked it what Harry had been looking into.

At first, Mr. Mime refused to talk. But after Tim mimed a few threats, the Pokémon gave them enough clues to figure it out. Mr. Mime nodded when Tim said, "Someone was handing out R, and the R came from the Roundhouse?"

Next, Tim and Detective Pikachu found the Roundhouse. It was a loud, crowded building—with a battle arena at the center. Tim gaped at the giant cage. "I didn't know they had Pokémon battles in Ryme City."

"They're not supposed to," Detective Pikachu said, shaking his head. As they poked around the arena, Detective Pikachu recapped what they knew. "So . . . Harry traced the vials of R here. Then he came here because someone knows something about something. We just need to find the someone . . . and the something."

CHARIZARD

"Hey!" A voice shouted over the loudspeaker. "Where's that Pikachu's partner?"

A tattooed guy wearing an oversize coat was pointing at them. Tim said, "I think the *someone* just found us."

"I'm Sebastian," The guy said, moving toward them. "Who are you?"

"I'm his . . . new partner," Tim said.

Sebastian snarled. "Well, that Pikachu's Thunderbolt almost wrecked my prized Charizard the last time he was here," he said. "Nobody comes into my place and does that to *my* Pokémon!"

"Look, I just want to know why his old partner was here," Tim said. "That's all."

Sebastian grinned. "You give me a rematch, I'll tell you everything you want to know."

"Tell him he's on." Detective Pikachu nodded at Tim. "Hold my hat. I've obviously dealt with his Charizard before."

Charizard and Detective Pikachu stepped into the battle arena. Sebastian told Charizard, "You're gonna win this time." Then he opened his coat. It was lined with vials of R! He popped one open and Charizard breathed in the strange gas.

Charizard burst into the center of the arena, looking totally crazed.

Detective Pikachu wailed, "That thing just chugged a year's worth of that R stuff!"

But it was too late. The battle was on.

Fired up, Charizard launched an attack. Tim told Detective Pikachu to use Volt Tackle as a move against Charizard, but he had forgotten how to use his powers!

Tim slipped into the cage and grabbed onto Charizard's tail to try to help his partner. "Pikachu, run!"

Detective Pikachu raced up Charizard's back and grabbed it by the eyelids.

Charizard spun around and around. Its tail sent Tim flying right into Sebastian, who had also entered the arena. Sebastian fell over, and all his vials of R shattered on the floor. Purple gas spread through the building. As the Pokémon in the crowd breathed it in, they all began to go *crazy*.

Sebastian tried to get away, but Tim held him down. "Tell me what you know!"

The guy you're looking for . . . He wanted to know the source of the R. It comes from the doctor," Sebastian said. "That's all I know!"

Tim and Detective Pikachu raced toward the exit, eager to escape the insane room full of crazed Pokémon. But Charizard was blocking the door. Detective Pikachu tossed a flopping Magikarp at it, and Magikarp evolved into a massive Gyarados. It shot out a mouthful of water—and blasted Tim and Detective Pikachu out onto the street!

A black SUV pulled up beside them. A woman in a dark suit gestured for them to get in. Without any other leads left to follow, Tim and Detective Pikachu agreed.

They were brought to the penthouse of the CNM building. Inside, an Eevee sat beside a man in shadows. As they walked toward it, the Eevee evolved into a Flareon.

"Imagine being able to evolve into the best possible version of yourself," the shadowed figure said. "Greatness inside you, just waiting to be awoken." The man rolled out of the shadows—it was Howard Clifford, the founder of Ryme City!

"Hello, Tim. I see you've partnered with Harry's Pikachu," Howard said.

"*You* knew Harry?" Tim said, shocked.

"The case Harry was working on—it was for me," Howard explained. "This compound called R threatens everything I've built. I hired Harry to trace it to its source. Imagine my shock when it turned out to be . . . my own son, Roger."

"That's a twist," Detective Pikachu muttered.

Howard went on, "Harry is the only one I can trust. That's why I need you to find him. Tim, your father is still alive."

Howard pressed a button and the walls around the office dissolved. Tim and Detective Pikachu were inside the scene of Harry's car accident. "Advanced holographic imaging," Howard explained.

Tim walked through the scene, stepping around his father's crashed car. Harry was lying on the ground. Alive, but barely. Beside him, a hologram of Detective Pikachu climbed out of the car.

"So, I was with Harry in the crash!" Detective Pikachu cried.

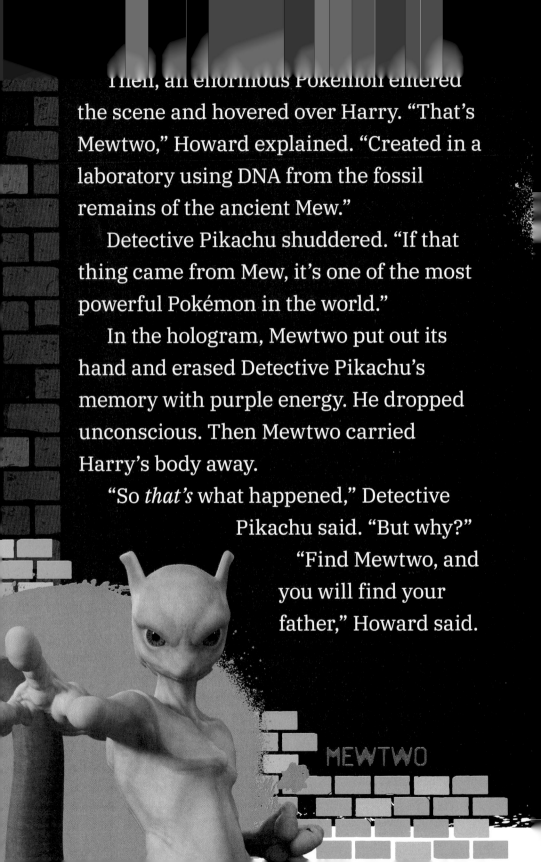

Then, an enormous Pokémon entered the scene and hovered over Harry. "That's Mewtwo," Howard explained. "Created in a laboratory using DNA from the fossil remains of the ancient Mew."

Detective Pikachu shuddered. "If that thing came from Mew, it's one of the most powerful Pokémon in the world."

In the hologram, Mewtwo put out its hand and erased Detective Pikachu's memory with purple energy. He dropped unconscious. Then Mewtwo carried Harry's body away.

"So *that's* what happened," Detective Pikachu said. "But why?"

"Find Mewtwo, and you will find your father," Howard said.

MEWTWO

Detective Pikachu and Tim had to figure out their next move. They found Lucy and filled her in, and she did some digging. Soon, she located a Pokémon Research Lab that had been paid for by the Clifford business!

"Last week, the lab had an 'accident' and had to shut down," she told Tim and Detective Pikachu. "This 'accident' was the same night Harry Goodman went missing." If they wanted answers, they would obviously have to visit that lab.

They all drove over to the lab, and Lucy and Psyduck led the group inside. They walked past all kinds of experiments that were in progress.

Dozens of Greninja were locked away in glass pods that were labeled POWER ENHANCEMENT. A bunch of Torterra were trapped inside a Torterra Garden that was labeled GROWTH ENHANCEMENT.

Whatever was being done to these Pokémon, it probably wasn't good.

While Lucy took photos of everything, Tim and Detective Pikachu stepped into a large, destroyed lab. At a desk labeled "Dr. Laurent," Detective Pikachu pressed a button on the computer, and a video hologram began.

This video took them on a tour of the history of the lab. "After much trial and error,

DR. LAURENT

we've perfected a stable method to extract Mewtwo's DNA," Dr. Laurent said in the video. She held up a purple vial. "We call this chemical serum *R*. Inhaling it results in a total loss of free will, and makes Pokémon go wild."

"She's 'the doctor'—they must have been testing R at the battles," Detective Pikachu said, horrified.

In the next segment of the video, Tim and Detective Pikachu watched as an angry-looking Mewtwo eyed Dr. Laurent from behind the glass. Suddenly, Mewtwo began to glow. It burst free from the chamber in an explosion of glass and purple energy!

The holographic recording ended suddenly. "That must have been how Mewtwo escaped from the lab," Tim said. "But what did it want with Harry?"

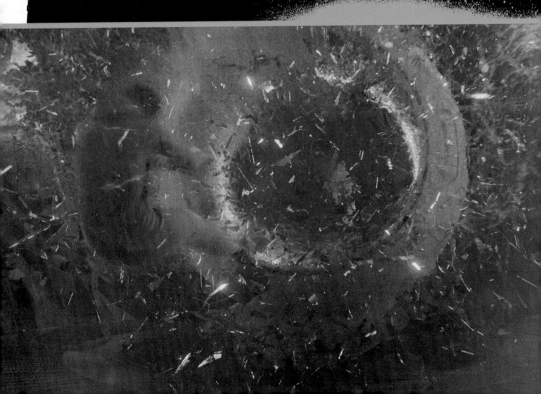

Tim and Detective Pikachu set off to find Lucy. But she was missing, and the enhanced Greninja pods were wide open.

"Lucy?" Tim called. A drop of slime hit the floor. He looked up. A Greninja was stuck to the ceiling, its tongue wrapped tightly around Lucy and Psyduck! Tim pulled the fire alarm on the wall. Startled, the Greninja let them go.

Lucy led the group into the Torterra Garden. At the back of the lab was a forest. They could escape through the trees!

"Something's wrong," Tim said suddenly. The ground was shaking.

Trees began smashing into one another. Suddenly, the ground spun out from under their feet, then split in half. Tim and Detective Pikachu were carried away from Lucy and Psyduck.

Detective Pikachu hopped up on Tim's shoulder as the ground began to crumble. "Kid, we have to do something—fast."

With a running leap, Tim jumped toward Lucy across the split ground.

Detective Pikachu clung to Tim's jacket as they flew through the air, then slammed down on the other side.

Detective Pikachu took a deep breath. "Phew. I thought I—I—EYEBALL!"

They all spun around. The boulder behind them had opened up and . . . was looking at them. "This isn't a forest at all," Detective Pikachu said. "This is a giant Torterra!"

Someone working in the lab had found a way to create *giant* Pokémon!

Suddenly, the giant Torterra started trying to shake the forest off its back. A rock flew through the air and hit Detective Pikachu in the head as the whole group slid off a ledge and landed in a lake below.

Tim carried an unconscious Detective Pikachu to shore. He saw a Bulbasaur at the forest's edge. "I need to get Pikachu help," he pleaded with it. "Please."

The Bulbasaur led Tim and Detective Pikachu deep into the forest. A voice called out, "I have been waiting for you." There, hovering above them, was Mewtwo.

BULBASAUR

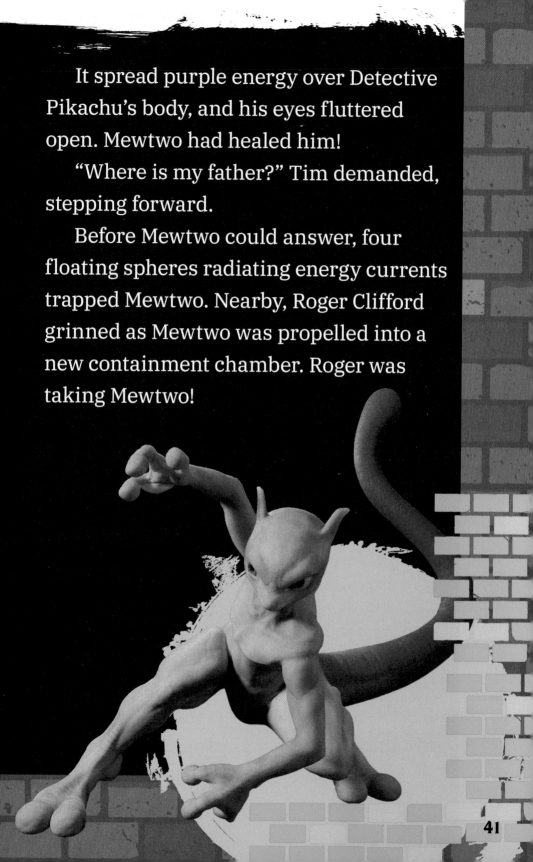

It spread purple energy over Detective Pikachu's body, and his eyes fluttered open. Mewtwo had healed him!

"Where is my father?" Tim demanded, stepping forward.

Before Mewtwo could answer, four floating spheres radiating energy currents trapped Mewtwo. Nearby, Roger Clifford grinned as Mewtwo was propelled into a new containment chamber. Roger was taking Mewtwo!

"Go on without me," Detective Pikachu said to Tim.

"What?" Tim asked, shocked. "But Roger has Mewtwo, and Mewtwo has my father. We have a case to solve. We've got to get back to the city."

Alone with his thoughts, Detective Pikachu set off in the opposite direction. There was something he needed to see . . .

While Tim and Lucy hustled back to the city, Detective Pikachu snooped around the scene of Harry's crash. Something still seemed fishy about the accident. Soon, he spotted something strange: Greninja throwing stars!

"Roger must have sent the Greninja to cause the crash," Detective Pikachu said. Of course! *Roger* had caused Harry's accident. Which meant Mewtwo had escaped to . . . try to protect him and Harry? Detective Pikachu wondered why Howard hadn't shown them that in the video. Unless . . . Howard was in on it!

Tim and Lucy got back to Ryme City just as the Tenth Anniversary City Pokémon Parade began. Giant Pokémon balloons floated over the streets. Everyone was downtown to celebrate.

Tim raced straight to Mr. Clifford's office . . . and found Howard by a containment chamber with Mewtwo trapped inside. As Tim watched, the chamber began to fill with purple R gas. A cable connected the chamber to Howard's head. Suddenly, Howard's body went limp. The chamber opened, and Mewtwo floated out.

"The transfer worked!" Howard boomed. He was speaking from inside Mewtwo's body. "My body is in the chair, but my mind is in Mewtwo!"

That's when Tim figured out what Detective Pikachu had. "*You* tried to kill Harry. Because he knew too much about R!" Tim said.

"Your father failed to understand my vision," Howard said. "Mewtwo has the power to transfer the mind of a human into the body of a Pokémon—as long as the Pokémon are in a crazed state from the R gas."

Tim gasped. "There's R gas in the parade balloons!" He tried to run out and warn people, but Howard blasted him aside.

Using his new Mewtwo body, Howard hovered over Ryme City. "I've finally discovered a cure," he boomed. "Not just for me, but for all humanity. Pokémon can evolve into better versions of themselves, and now, so can you." Using his powers, he opened valves on the giant balloons, releasing R gas over the crowd.

All over the city, Pokémon began to go crazy. Then, one by one, every human's mind was transferred into their Pokémon partner's body.

Meanwhile, Detective Pikachu returned to the city. Lucy in Psyduck's body tried to explain what was going on.

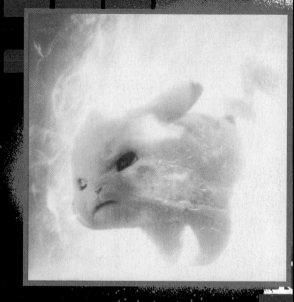

"Howard *is* Mewtwo?" Detective Pikachu gasped. "I've gotta stop this!"

Tim glanced out the window of Clifford Tower and saw Detective Pikachu riding on the back of a giant Pidgeot, battling Mewtwo. Tim realized he had to take his chance while Howard was distracted by Detective Pikachu. He raced toward the cable connecting Howard's head to the chamber—and he pulled the plug.

Just like that, Howard Clifford's mind returned to his human body.

"Please tell me you can fix this mess," Detective Pikachu said to Mewtwo, now that Mewtwo was back in control of itself.

Mewtwo nodded and released an enormous purple blast. All the humans and Pokémon returned to their normal forms.

"There is one last thing I must fix," Mewtwo said. It had tried to help Harry because Harry had tried to help Pokémon. "After the accident, this Pikachu offered his body to save Harry's mind. I took the body to keep it safe. But I can now repair him."

Mewtwo shot a *whoosh* of energy . . . and where Detective Pikachu had been standing there now stood both Pikachu and Harry!